The McKinley Street Ghost

Other books written by Edeth Hamm

"The Antics of Addison and Winston from A to Z"

*Parenting 101: Ten Throwback Steps to Raising a
Responsible Child
(By Someone Who Has Never Been a Parent)

Trafford Publishing
Victoria, BC Canada

****

"4th Grade Language Arts"

Teaching Point Publishing

The McKinley Street Ghost

By edeth hamm

Order this book online at www.trafford.com
or email orders@trafford.com

Most Trafford titles are also available at major online book retailers.

Printed in Victoria, BC, Canada.

ISBN: 978-1-4269-1485-0

*Our mission is to efficiently provide the world's finest, most
comprehensive book publishing service, enabling every author to
experience success. To find out how to publish your book, your way, and
have it available worldwide, visit us online at www.trafford.com*

Trafford rev. 12/18/2009

 www.trafford.com

North America & international
toll-free: 1 888 232 4444 (USA & Canada)
phone: 250 383 6864 ♦ fax: 812 355 4082

**To all of my 4th graders
who helped critique this book**

Preface

It has been difficult for people to believe that I actually grew up in a 'haunted' house. I wish that I was making it up, but it is true. Back in the days of my childhood, the town that we moved to was relatively small, so once you rented or purchased a house, you were pretty much 'stuck' there unless you moved to another town. Vacancy signs were just about non-existent.

It was my mother's patience and fortitude and tenaciousness that taught us about fear and how to 'overcome' it. Although some of the events have been 'sensationalized' for your reading pleasure, much of what you read is how it actually happened. Of course, I have changed names and characterizations to protect the innocent.

Table of Contents

Chapter One A Moving Experience   1

Chapter Two "The Haunting"   6

Chapter Three Ghost Writer   11

Chapter Four More Strange Occurrences   14

Chapter Five The Birthday Party   20

Chapter Six The Woods   25

Chapter Seven Our Mystery Fire   28

Chapter Eight In the Attic   33

Chapter Nine The Decision   35

Chapter Ten IT's Back   40

Chapter Eleven Telling Books   42

Chapter Twelve The Plan   46

Chapter Thirteen Exorcising a Ghost   48

Chapter Fourteen Waiting   53

Chapter Fifteen The Ghastly Truth   57

Chapter Sixteen Leaving McKinley Street   60

Poems

The McKinley Street Ghost   12

Invisible Footsteps   17

The Woods   25

Decision Maker   37

Telling Books   44

Ghost Notes   56

Steel Mill Ashes and Grave Dust   59

The Year for the Child   65

Introduction

Deedra Pope, a quiet sensitive, bespectacled, twelve year-old, wanted to be taken more seriously about what she saw and heard in and around the house her family had moved into three years ago. It was hard to convince them that a ghost crept into the house every night while they were all asleep. Clara Pope felt these ghost stories were another figment of her daughter's vivid imagination, especially since she had a special gift for creating stories and writing poetry. Her father, Frank, was always too tired to care, and her siblings didn't want to hear about such spooky things. After three years of a series of frightful events, Deedra was finally able to persuade her family to become believers. In fact, they waited until it was almost too late. Only Deedra can tell the story the way it really unfolded...

Background

Milltown, a rural town in northern Indiana, is nestled in the middle of the industrial area where Mr. Pope had landed a job in the steel mill. The mill's towering smokestacks and billowing gray smog served as a backdrop for the downtown area. Just about everybody in that town work there. They melt iron, make steel structures, and sweep little mounds of ashes from the walkways that belch out of the smoke stacks all day long. Sometimes the ashes hover over City Hall (and a few other tall brick buildings nearby) like huge dark clouds waiting for dusk to creep in, before they gently rain down on the buildings and grass below. Needless to say, they blacken everything in their paths on Main Street.

Main Street cuts the city right in half. On the east side of town are plenty of two-story brick buildings and single-family dwellings that look just alike. Far away from the downtown area to the west are vacant lots, clumps of fir trees and open fields full of sand dunes and tall grasses that make that side of Milltown pretty ordinary. It's not exactly city life, neither is it country life. Further north are the rich people who run the town during the day but escape its pollution in the evening and night. Folks can easily find their way around Milltown, because on the east side of Main the streets are named after the states in the order that they entered the Union. The west side streets are named after the presidents in the order that they served in the White House. William Taft McKinley Street was where Mr. Pope and his family had settled.

****

Chapter One
A Moving Experience

<u>August 1967</u> My father, Frank Pope, was an honest, hardworking man, about 6 feet tall and a muscular build, with a receding hairline mingled with grey. He had grown up on a small Southern farm where he practically worked from sunup to sundown to help his family make do. Sometimes he would miss going to school during harvest season, because all hands were needed to make sure that no crops were lost. My dad secretly vowed that he wouldn't do this kind of work for the rest of his life—not the working hard part—but the farming. He vowed that once he had a wife and family of his own, that he would go looking for a better way of life to support them. He was the sole breadwinner in our household of seven. He had heard that they were hiring laborers in the local steel mill and the pay was good. So the entire family-- my father, my mother, Clara, my big brother Bud, my older sister Betty, and my two younger brothers, Jacob and Sam packed up everything and moved up North to Milltown.

Clara Pope, my mother, was a soft-spoken matronly type who absolutely adored her children. She dutifully took care of all of us without complaint. I marveled at how she kept everyone and everything in place, while cooking and cleaning and counseling all at the same time. My big brother, Bud, was outgoing and carefree. He helped out sometimes around the house, but his biggest job was to tend to his pet rooster and hens, and rabbits, and our dog, Tampa. My sister, Betty, was my best friend; we had each other's backs. She was only a year and a half older than me, so we thought alike in a lot of ways. But, in a lot of ways we were different. She was more active and agile; her biggest desire was to make the cheerleading squad. Jacob was a year older than Sam, who was eight years younger than me. They were the usual rough and tough boys, who liked sports and playing stick ball in the street. Betty and I had to help our mother look after them since they had come along later in her life, just when her energy level was starting to decline. We didn't mind so much, because we loved them a lot.

I thought of myself as a typical nine-year old, but closer to the nerdy type who was shy, wore glasses and kept my hair braided in pigtails. Most of my time was spent reading books, drawing, writing short stories and poems. Unlike Betty, I preferred being in the background where I could just observe and take everything in.

I was complimented a lot on being a quick study, so it didn't take me long to learn the layout of Milltown. On the east side on Main Street, which split the town in half, were the United States streets-- Delaware would be the first east side street, followed by Pennsylvania, then New Jersey and on down the line. On *our* side of Main, streets were named after the United States Presidents. By no means were we any more diplomatic than the state- side folks, but the streets were named in the order that each president served their country. You know, Washington, Adams, Jefferson, Madison, Monroe, Jackson, and so forth and so on. Except if two presidents had the same last name, only one name got used. About twenty-two blocks away was William Taft McKinley Street, named after the 25th president of the United States, the street where we had moved. For me this place was not so ordinary, and it didn't take my mother long to size up the folks we would be sharing McKinley Street with. I always felt she had a sixth sense about her, because she was as solid as a rock in her judgment about people.

"Kids, I don't ever want to see you go into the Trepples' house," she warned us the first week we moved there. "Never eat anything from those people," she continued.

My mother now seemed to be talking to herself. "I can't quite put my finger on it, but something's not right about them. I've met the neighbors on either side of us and on the corner up on the avenue; they all seem to be pretty decent, but I wonder about the Trepples."

Mr. and Mrs. Trepple lived almost directly across the street from us. Mrs. Trepple, a rather tall, unkempt woman, with mingled gray hair, was also a stay-at-home mom. Mr. Trepple was about two feet shorter than she was which added to their oddity. He usually seemed in a hurry going to get to work at the mill and when he returned home. They had a nine-year old daughter, one middle boy, and two older boys. All day long the front door of their house would be left wide open to allow stray cats that hung around the house to saunter in and out at will. Buzzing black flies swarmed in and out just as freely as the cats. Every morning a dirty white goat grazed in the tall grassy lot on one side of their house, while three dirty white spotted pigs grunted in an illegal makeshift sty in the back yard. An old rusty broken-down gutted blue van was parked out front with two flat tires. The stray cats had access to it as well. A mangy dog was a permanent fixture in front of the van waiting for someone to throw him a bone or some scraps of food. The two oldest boys, Jessie and William, hung out in it everyday after school and on weekends. Rumor had it that it was their clubhouse, and when they got sick of hearing their mom yelling at them, they would hide out in it. All I knew was that I had to stay away from *it* and *them.*

Across the other side of the dusty avenue were Mr. and Mrs. Cott and their twelve-year old twin girls, Marla and Carla. They lived in the only three-story house on the block. It had a basement, the main floor, and the upstairs. This gave them the advantage of peeping out at the neighbors from every level, and they did a lot of that. Every time I went outside to play, I could see someone peering out of one of the windows. The few times I would see the twins playing in their backyard for short periods, as soon as they spotted me, they would retreat back inside. After a month or so, my mom allowed me go over there to play since she knew that I wouldn't be gone long. Even though the Cotts appeared to be the nosiest neighbors on the block, they seemed pretty nice, or pretended to be anyway.

Our house was quite dreary. Rough dark green shingles covered it from the flat roof to just above the concrete basement. The 'Upstairs' had a wooden porch that went around one end of the front of the house; the back porch was quite small with very steep wooden stairs.

At ground level four concrete steps led down into the basement where the Burnsides lived, an elderly eccentric couple who were our landlords. They had retired after their son joined the Army, and then moved into the basement so they could rent the 'Upstairs' to supplement their income. Once inside of the 'Upstairs,' there was a great room that served as a parlor- living room with a large picture window that faced the street. On one end of the house were two bedrooms and a bathroom. On the other end was a kitchen and a huge pantry big enough to hold a washing machine and the shelves for canned goods.

My mother and father slept in one of the bedrooms, and the three boys slept in the other. The girls had to sleep in the living room area on the let-out couch. On snowy days we couldn't play inside, because our landlords could hear every squeak and cracking sound that the old hardwood floors made. I figured after working thirty long years at the steel mill had obviously begun to wear on their nerves, because they seemed to complain about every crack that was made over their heads when we walked from one room to the other. So, we had to sit still and watch television a lot. This quiet time didn't bother me as much, because I could concentrate on my writing. But it was really tough on my younger brothers. Whenever Jacob and Sam did chance to turn their bed into a trampoline to see who could touch the ceiling first with their head, Mrs. Burnside would take her broomstick and knock on her basement ceiling, yelling to them to cut the noise out. I grew to hate that house, and sometimes I thought I hated Mrs. Burnside.

Chapter Two
"The Haunting"

September 1967 Haunted houses are supposed to be old, deserted mansions, standing high on a hilltop with spider webs draped over the doors and windows, where every now and then a pair of piercing yellow eyes peeps through a cracked pane. But this house was not like that; it was alive and full of events. With a stay-home mother, a father who would work long hours at the mill but reached home in time for a late dinner, and five energetic children, a lot went on throughout the day that kept any strange occurrences from ever being detected. It was at night, though, when everyone had settled down for bed and all the lights were off, that this old house *really* came alive.

After living there for less than a month, I knew the house was haunted. Most evenings during the summer, I kept a window slightly open to let the night breeze cool down the room where Betty and I slept. Just as the sun would sink below the beautiful scarlet veil, I began to listen closely to all of the strange sounds that invaded the neighborhood— eerie sounds that penetrated the wooden walls inside the house—squeaky noises, moaning, heavy breathing, and heavy footsteps.

"Hey, Dee!" my tomboy sister took my attention away as I watched the sun slowly sink down below the horizon. "I've got bids on the inside of the bed again tonight!" she insisted.

The inside of the bed meant sleeping on the side of the pull-out sofa that touched the wall, which would leave me on the outside next to the open dark space where the ghost would make its silent stand. *Watching over me?* Perhaps. *Frightening me?* Of course. During those nightly visitations, even on the hottest nights, my sister and I would cover our heads with a sheet or blanket and sweat profusely. Some nights, those pigs would start squealing and wouldn't stop. I could hear a chain dragging on the ground, as heavy footsteps stomped in the dusty street. Just as quickly as those unnerving sounds began they would suddenly stop. This was the beginning of what would become many sleepless nights for me.

Slam! The sound of a heavy car door [like a sliding van door] would always pierce the night calm. The pigs would begin to nervously grunt and escalate up to a shrill squeal, as the steady trudging of feet could be heard crossing the street. Slowly and deliberately the sound continued up our driveway, approaching the house. Methodically, IT moved on to the back of the house and up the steep back stairs.

Er-r-r—the creaky wooden back door squeaked as the nightly visitor stealthily allowed ITself in.

Er-r-r—IT would always shut the door behind him. C-crack, c-crack, c-crack—the squeaky wooden floor would give way to the weight of ITs footsteps—from the pantry, through the kitchen, into the living room, and finally, up to where I was sleeping.

Questions would bombard my brain like a hailstorm in mid-August. *'What did IT want? Why was IT in the house? Why couldn't IT leave?'* Silently I would pray for morning, for the return of the sunlight and the sweet chattering of the birds, my only salvation from those incredibly dark and sleepless nights.

No one believed me when I'd tell them about the house being haunted, they insisted it was my vivid imagination and my often insomnia. If I could just get someone to stay up long enough with me to hear what I was hearing, then I would know that I wasn't losing my mind—but there were no takers. Did I ever see anything? If I had, I wouldn't be able to tell about it, because IT would've killed me. In fact, 'IT' almost did.

****

Interlude

Cockadoo-la-doo! Cockadoo-la-roo! Charlie was Bud's majestic banter rooster whose shiny feathers seemed to have more colors than a rainbow. About six o'clock every morning he would send out a shrill cry so loud over the twenty-three hundred block of McKinley Street that it would wake up the neighborhood and the morning sun. His early rising meant he had to tend to his seven speckled brown hens that constantly laid eggs for him. He would strut around the backyard as he continued his crooning for an hour like he was *the King of the Hill, the Ruler of the Roost, the McKinley Street Pride.* Nothing frightened Charlie; he was a great fighter with razor-sharp talons and a curved fierce beak. He would charge after anyone or anything that would come near his harem—even Clara Pope didn't get his respect. Bud was the only one who could go inside the coup to collect those delicate brown eggs. Charlie was on his watch twenty-four hours, always sleeping with one eye open. Yet I couldn't quite understand how he never heard the dark intruder mounting the back steps up to the lofty porch every night, he never squawked one time. Either Mr. Rooster didn't hear or see IT, or he was too afraid to make a sound.

"Morning, Dee, did you get a good night's sleep this time, or did that imagination of yours get the best of you again?" My mother chuckled with her usual light-hearted humor. She still had trouble understanding why her youngest daughter couldn't go soundly asleep each night.

"Never mind that I didn't sleep a wink, dear Mama. Just never you mind," I muttered under my breath.

My mother laughed harder this time. "Honey, I just wish you could get this silliness out of your head. There's nothing that can come through that back door, I make sure it's locked at night. When I check it in the morning, it's still locked. You tell me, what could possibly come through a locked back door?"

Since my mother didn't really believe in ghosts, it was useless to go into my explanation again that IT could walk *through* doors. Even though I would hear the door open and close, I had to admit that I couldn't quite explain why it would still be locked the next morning. No signs of forced entry, nothing missing, everything intact. The minute doubt would start to creep in to persuade me to believe that it *was* my imagination, a little voice in my head kept me convinced of what I heard at night.

"Hey, Dee, did the boogey man visit you again last night, huh?" It was Betty who asked the question this time.

It always amazed me how easily Betty would play it off like it was *my* problem only. She was just as afraid as I was, that's why she always jumped at the chance for the inside of the bed against the wall. Unlike me, however, she would fall asleep quickly. Anyway, I wasn't going to get into another argument with my sister about her hypocrisy; I had to get ready for school. For the next three years, I would have many sleepless, hot nights—shaking under the covers, even in the summer time. I was convinced that so far, they were the worst years of my life.

Chapter Three
Ghost Writer

September 1970 English was my first period class in sixth grade at the local high school. As the tardy bell was about to ring, I rushed in to put my books down on my desk and sharpen my pencils. *Ring! Ring! Ring!* My teacher, Miss Engle, promptly began calling roll. The morning assignment was already written on the board.

Write a poem about an unusual occurrence in your family. The poem does not have to rhyme, although I would encourage a light, humorous couplet.

I liked school a lot, especially my English class, because I got to do what I do best--write. Miss Engle, a first-year teacher and a published writer herself, would encourage us to write about our fun, personal experiences, this way it would be easier to think of ideas and topics. But, every time I tried to be fresh and delightful, I could only think of the dark side of my life--the ghost on my street that had been creeping into our house and invading my sleep for the past three years. When I picked up my pencil to force myself to write about how much I enjoyed fun times with my family, my hand seemed to move by itself.

The McKinley Street Ghost

Nightly footsteps still and steady
Tread upon a wooden floor
Drowning out the darkness, ready
To enter in through my bolted back door

"What do you want of me?" I asked forlorn
Each night I sweat and quiver under my covers
Praying that I will awake by morn
While the tall dark figure watches and hovers

When morning peeks through tattered tapestry
I slowly creep out of my makeshift tomb
Glad to see that I'm set free
From being held hostage in my own room.

Every writing assignment I would try to write something light and fun, but instead I would go on and on and on about this 'Thing' that was haunting me, this 'Thing' that had completely taken over my thoughts—and lately my writing hand.

"Deedra Pope!" my teacher would exclaim. "Why are your poems and your stories always about this silly notion that you live in a haunted house? Poetry and prose is more than gloom and doom, child," she continued. Come on, write about happy things. I'm sure you must have a happy side to your life!"

I knew Miss Engle was trying to encourage me to become a better writer, and I was trying, but IT wouldn't let me. I wanted to tell her how my mother is the love of my life, how my sister, Betty, is my constant companion and confidante. How my older brother makes me feel secure and safe when he's around and how my two younger brothers keep me active and responsible. I certainly wanted to gloat about my ex- military father who worked long hours to take care of all of us. Instead, my thoughts were drawn to more desperate, unfriendly things.

I wanted to tell her about the time my two brothers saw a baby with yellow eyes crawl into their bed one night. When they described it to my mother the next morning, to our surprise, she hesitantly admitted that it fit the description of her first-born son who died of yellow jaundice when he was only six months old. There were no pictures taken of him, so my brothers had never seen him before. I wanted to tell Miss Engle about the slamming of the old van door most nights, the pigs squealing, and the nightly footsteps that came into our house. Since she already thought it was a *silly notion* that I lived on a street that was haunted and in a house that was haunted, I knew that I would have trouble convincing her of what I was experiencing—so I didn't answer. Somehow, someway I would have to eventually get my message across to someone who did believe.

Chapter Four
More Strange Occurrences

October 1970 I was determined to make this Thing that was taking over my life come forward and identify ITself or to just go away. Out of desperation, I began keeping a diary on all the strange events, the dates and times of these occurrences to see if there was a pattern. I went all the way back to three years ago when we first moved into the house. Maybe I'd be able to track IT that way, or at least learn how to avoid its evil presence. Well, interestingly enough, the next six weeks passed fairly uneventful, as if IT was trying to throw me off somehow. This was a time of my vulnerability and confusion-- my family had begun to convince me that I was wildly imaginative and this had all been a bad dream. Just as I was about to give in to their theory of me having nightmares, something strange happened in broad daylight. One Saturday afternoon, my mother, Sam, Jacob, Betty and I were sitting on the oversized front porch chatting away, when all of a sudden Jessie, the oldest Trepple boy, flung the sliding door of the van open, slammed it shut, and came running out whooping like a wild frightened whooping crane.

"Whoop! Whoop!" He charged through the open door of his house and slammed it behind him shut. Shortly after, Mrs. Trepple came to the window and pushed the torn curtain aside. She looked curiously at the van as if she was trying to see what was in it. When she spotted us on the porch, she quickly closed the curtain. My mother shooed us in the house, mumbling about not wanting us to see the likes of that crazy kid across the street. To avoid our wide-eyed expressions and any ensuing questions we had, she turned on the TV and retreated to the kitchen to start dinner.

No matter how much my mother had tried to downplay that scene, I couldn't relax at all. The sight of Jessie Trepple running out of that van kept replaying in my head; I couldn't forget how frightened he was. What had he seen to make him run like a bat out of Hades? That question stood out the most in my mind. What had he seen?

After that episode, we didn't see Jessie Trepple for over a month. Rumor had it that he couldn't speak for weeks, all he ever did was grunt. He couldn't tell anyone what he had seen, nor could he describe it in writing. Eventually he drew a picture of a very hideous looking man with wiry hair, flaming eyes, and he held a shiny machete with both hands. When I did finally see Jessie emerge from the house, he made sure he stayed at least fifty feet away from the van, avoiding it like the bubonic plague. I remembered my mother's warning about staying away from them. "Maybe this is what she was talking about," I thought out loud.

Anyway, that same night after his incident, I suspected stranger things would happen, and I wasn't disappointed.

Again, everyone had fallen asleep but me. The street had a weird dead silence to it; I believe that I was the only one awake in the whole neighborhood.

Bam! The heavy metal van door slammed open and then shut jolting me up in a sitting position on the side of the couch.

"*Woof! Woof! Woof!*" This time it was not the noise of squealing pigs afraid of the night stalker, but of fearless barking dogs aimed to protect their turf. (I'm convinced that animals have a keener sense than humans do about the invisible world.) The heavy trudging hesitated, and then continued up the driveway to our house. The dogs began to gnash and gash their sharp teeth. Suddenly, unmistakable sounds of heavy footsteps began to run on the ground, pounding hard on the asphalt, then round and round the house. I jumped up and dashed over to the window to peer out through a tear in the curtain, determined to finally get a glimpse of this ruthless character. The footsteps became harder and louder, but I saw no one—only the two family dogs and a neighbor's dog as they flashed by. Three times around Blackie, Tampa, and Callie fiercely ran at full speed behind *something*, yelping loudly as they went. On the third round, the footsteps headed out to the woods behind the house; the snarling dogs boldly followed. With no time to get my glasses from the coffee table, I stumbled to the kitchen to peer out through the back window. Barely able to see in the dim moonlight, I grimaced. There IT was. I could faintly make out a tall dark figure of a man hazily outlined against the misty background of the trees. He whirled around, swiftly raised both hands up in the air holding on to what looked like a silver machete, ready to strike the dogs if they came closer.

"Ow! Ow! Ow!" The dogs cried out. I ran for my glasses and returned as fast as I could to the window. They made a sharp turn towards the house; their piercing cries became louder as they approached the back stairs. Neither of them stopped until they had safely reached the top of the porch. With their tails tucked between their legs, these three vicious dogs had suddenly been turned into limp, frightened, whimpering pooches. I knew then that Blackie, Tampa and Callie had seen IT too. The dark stranger spotted me in the window, we exchanged glances. I stood motionless, mesmerized, and afraid to move until I saw the shadowy shape stealthily vanish deep into the woods. I was mortified and equally petrified.

Invisible Footsteps

Footsteps running fast
Pass the windows
Around and around
Hard on the ground

Brave dogs
Panting and yapping
Running after IT
Tongues wagging, hair
standing
Trying to protect their
turf

But IT

Frightened even them
Led them to the edge
Of the woods
To turn and appear to them
As only something
hideous could

Sent those brave dogs
Running affright
Tails between their
legs
On that cold dark
Night.

The next day when I arrived home from school, I found the front door slightly ajar. I called out to my mother, but there was no answer. No one was home, which was very unusual.

"She and the boys were probably visiting next door," I thought out loud. When I slowly walked in, I felt the hair stand up on my arms. There was Callie, our neighbor's collie-mix, sitting on the couch with a blank stare on his face as if in a trance.

"Callie!" I yelled at him. "What are you doing in our house? You know you're not allowed in here! Mama's going to have a fit!" I moved closer to him, but he wouldn't budge. Callie has never been a feely-touchy kind of dog, yet I had a crazy impulse to come even closer to give him a hug. The hair stood up on his back as he began to growl at me, his eyes had turned a fire engine red.

I jumped back and ran out to the porch. Nervously, I waited on the steps until my mother and the boys came home from next door. When I told her about Callie, she bravely walked in and shooed him outside without incident. As he went pass me, he looked up and whined as if apologizing for offending me.

This was obviously bigger than me—and my family. Even the family pets can't protect us, I thought. What was I going to do? How could I convince my parents to move as far away from this wretched place as we could? I would need another person to see and hear what the dogs and I—and even Jessie Trepple had seen and heard. Again, who would be brave enough to come forth?

****

Chapter Five
The Birthday Party

November 1970 "Happy birthday to you!" Mrs. Cott, Betty, and I sang to the twins on their 13th birthday. Marla and Carla were identical twins. With the exception of a mole on the left side of Marla's nose, you couldn't tell them apart.

When we first moved to the neighborhood, it took us a while to warm up to them, because their parents were very strict about allowing them to come out to play. The only way we got to spend quality time with the twins was when we ate lunch together at school. Marla often complained about having to do most of the housework and how Carla only had to help out in the kitchen at dinner time. They both were attractive girls, but Carla had a more inviting face, she smiled a lot, which seemed to be infectious. More kids wanted to sit near her at lunch to hear her tell intriguing stories about strange things that happened in their house. Marla rarely took part in chirping about their personal lives, she was shy and reserved, preferring to chit chat about a book she was reading or an assignment she had been given in her English class. Sometimes, Betty and I would walk home from school with them, but they would move over to the other side of the street when we got closer to McKinley Street. They weren't allowed to walk with other kids— only with each other. So it surprised me when Mrs.Cott had invited Betty and me over for punch, hot sweetbread and vanilla ice cream at their birthday party.

Unlike her daughters, Mrs. Cott, a heavy built middle aged woman, was quite outgoing in the neighborhood. She seemed to know personal business from every household on our street. She spent a lot of time standing in her yard talking to Mrs. Trepple, who frequented her at least three times a week. I was curious about how they seemed to keep a watchful eye on our house. They would talk awhile, then look over at the house, then turn to each other and talk some more. Sometimes an hour would go by before I would get up from the porch to go into the house, leaving them to talk again.

The two girls made a wish, and then simultaneously blew out the thirteen candles on the square-layered sweetbread with vanilla icing spread on top. We clapped our hands and Betty and I gave each of them a hug. We started up a light chatter while Mrs. Cott cut the square cake; Marla started scooping ice cream from the half-gallon carton waiting in the kitchen sink. Carla poured the red punch in little glasses that came with the glass punch bowl. I anxiously waited for my first taste.

Without warning there was a strange noise at the back door as if someone was trying to unlatch the screen door. Slowly the squeaky door began to crack open. We were hoping it was Mr. Cott, a tall, stout, slow-walking man, coming in from outside to join the party, but no one entered. The happy chatter stopped, the five of us were frozen with curiosity. Gradually footsteps walked through the kitchen, passed by our group gathered around the table, continued out to the living room, and to the front door. The front screen door swung open and slammed shut. We stood with our eyes bucked and our mouths hanging open.

"Oh my, it's a good thing we got a good gust of wind to come through, we certainly could use a little cooling down." Mrs. Cott broke the silence.

I couldn't believe that she brushed that off as if it hadn't happened. *Gusts of wind don't cause footsteps to walk through your house,* I wanted to correct her, but I had been taught to respect my elders. My mind started racing--*Is IT following me or had it walked through the Cotts' kitchen before?* Could this be one of those strange occurrences that Carla was telling us about at lunch? The one she called— her secret? Even if Mrs. Cott is trying to dismiss the incident as coincidental, at least Betty was a witness to what I'd been trying to tell her and my family about for years.

"Psst, did you hear what I heard?" I whispered in her ear. She ignored me but asked the twins if this had happened before, which let me know that she had heard it too. Marla just stared wide-eyed, seemingly afraid to answer; it was obvious that she just didn't want to talk about it either.

I couldn't take the hush-hush attitudes of everyone, so I abruptly broke in, "Mrs. Cott, I think I'd better run home before it gets too dark. Happy Birthday Carla and Marla!" I thanked them for the invite, asked Betty if she was coming with me. She shyly lingered there, looking embarrassed. My sister could play brave if she wanted to, but I wasn't about to pretend that I wasn't scared out of my wits. I no longer cared about the sweetbread and the ice cream or the punch. I politely excused myself at the back door and bounded down the stairs as fast as I could.

"But Deedra, you didn't eat your sweetbread and ice cream! Mrs. Cott yelled from the porch. "Come back so we can pray about this, child!"

Running at full speed I never looked back. I didn't even bother to look both ways before dashing across the avenue. At this point I didn't even care that I was being rude to Mrs. Cott, to Marla and Carla and certainly not to my sister. All I knew was that I had to get out of that house as quickly as I could and back to a safer haven. Yes, I felt safer in *my* haunted house than in someone else's.

Just as I reached the top of the back stairs, the phone was ringing—I yelled that I would get it. It was Betty asking me to meet her at the edge of the avenue, because she was too afraid to head for home alone. Feeling sorry for her, I went just halfway to the edge of the street until I saw her running towards me. She said that Mr. Cott had come inside after I left. They all had compromised that he was playing a prank on us. I told her that she could try to explain away what just happened, but to count me out. I knew what I had seen and heard and no one was going to change my mind about it.

Later that evening, our dogs began to howl uncontrollably. They had heard the fire sirens peeling in the quiet humid night air long before we did. The closer the fire truck approached, the louder the peel got and the louder the dogs howled.

I could tell that the fire truck and ambulance were getting nearer to McKinley Street, but I didn't know why.

Rarely did we hear fire trucks or police cars in our quiet neighborhood; just slamming van doors and squealing pigs at night. The noise from the trucks became deafening as we could hear screeching tires making a sharp turn onto our street—but it was a right turn. Everyone ran out into the yard but me to find out what all of the commotion was about. The night air was cold and damp--we couldn't believe our eyes.

Fire was blazing from the Cott's kitchen windows on the second floor. From where I was on my porch, I could see the twins standing by the road in their night robes clutching each other and crying. Mr. Cott stood closer to the yard with his arm around his wife, staring in disbelief. Mrs. Cott was weeping heavily. Thank goodness everybody had gotten out in time. It took the firefighters over an hour to put the blaze out. All the neighbors stood in their yards watching and gossiping about what had started the fire, but no one had a really good explanation.

After the fire, we didn't see the twins or Mr. and Mrs. Cott for a week. We saw inspectors from the fire department going in and out of their house for a couple of days, we also saw a van parked in the driveway over several days with Jake's Plumbing and Flooring painted on both sides of the vehicle. When I did see Marla at lunch again, she told me that they had moved in with their aunt on Roosevelt Street until the smoke had cleared the house. She went on to say that they would move into their basement for about a month until the upstairs was repaired and painted. I was convinced that all these strange events were connected in some way to our surprise uninvited guest at the birthday party. I was also convinced that this was not the first time *IT* had visited them.

Chapter Six

The Woods

Tall elms, leafy oaks, and acorn trees
Stand so stately in staggered rows
Leafy headdresses create a
special canopy
Trapping the sunlight and
allowing it to filter through
At intervals.

Flowers dot the forest floor
Whimsically dancing in the often breeze
While fallen leaves scurry about
Looking for a place to quietly lay
Only to decay when winter comes

December 1970 Weeks had passed since the birthday party, the 'sighting,' and the fire. I started feeling safe again when I cut through the woods in back of my house. Not only was it a shorter way home from school, it gave me time to be alone to escape my problems. Although the tall trees kept out most of the sunlight, I enjoyed the tranquility and solitude that the semi-darkness would bring. Here I didn't think about ghosts, but I would allow myself to become one with nature. I especially loved the little furry creatures that skittered and scurried about in the undergrowth that grew around the base of the trees. Fuzzy brown squirrels, black and white rabbits, birds of every kind, and even a few raccoons seemed to play hide-n-seek with each other; while bugs, garter snakes and lots of field mice made their home in those woods too. I found my favorite tree stump, dropped my books on the ground and sat down. A light breeze stirred some of the dried leaves laying on the ground, while live leaves rustled gently overhead. I took in a deep breath of oxygen from the greenery that surrounded me and began to chat with a little squirrel I had named Chestnut. He had grown to trust me, so he came very close to the stump to eat the bread crust I had saved for him from my lunch. Whenever the other animals would see me, they would make all kinds of happy sounds as they hurried about, but only Chestnut dared to come close.

Strangely, the wind began to sweep around the trees disturbing everything in its path. An old jagged forked oak tree branch was flung over to the edge of the wood from the strength of the wind. The leaves began rustling noisily, many falling to the ground as they were tossed to and fro. A streak of lightning flashed in the distance, a thunderous roar seemed to shake the entire forest. I sat motionless, sensing the worst was on its way as the dark luminous clouds began to overcast the sunlight.

I could smell the freshness from the raindrops even before the first one hit my cheek. The drops picked up speed, the lightning flashed quicker. One after the other, the enormous thunderous roars accompanied each electrifying streak. I stood up, but it was hopeless to try to run for the house, everything was already too fierce, so

I stumbled further back into the woods where the trees made a canopy over me. I knew I would stay dry, but I also knew that lightning could strike a tree with any one of the sharp flashes across the sky. Worse still, I could get struck by one of the strikes that hit the ground between the woods and the back door. I felt afraid and trapped, but I could only wait until it was safe to make a run to the back stairs. In some strange way, I trusted that the trees would protect me. But in a stranger way, I felt that I was not in the woods alone, that I was being watched. Momentarily, I was unable to see through the approaching darkness, but when the time was right, I dodged through the heavy raindrops to the back stairway. Like the dogs that unforgettable night, I bounded the stairs and ran into the house without looking back.

That night after the darkness had completely fallen upon the rooftops, the streets, and eventually engulfed the whole neighborhood, something would leave those woods to pay us a visit. It would be one of the most horrifying nights of all.

Chapter Seven
Our Mystery Fire

"Mama, have fun, don't worry about us. We'll be fine!" Betty assured her.

It was a very rare occasion that our mother ever went out at night just to get away. She was the ultimate mother hen, her children were her life. Besides, by sundown she would be so exhausted from all the things that mothers do, she would retire to bed early. But this time we insisted that she go to a movie or something. As usual, my father was working late again and couldn't take her, but two of her close friends were going to pick her up and drop her back home after the show. Bud had another one of his hot dates, which meant Betty and I had to baby sit Jacob and Sam.

The four of us had the house all to ourselves. We watched a couple of our favorite shows on television for another hour before it was bedtime for the boys. After tucking them into bed, I curled up with my favorite book, *Black Beauty*, while Betty continued to watch TV. With the exception of the low talking from the television program, the house seemed unusually quiet for early evening, but I didn't think much of it. Every now and then we would hear squeaking and tiny feet scurrying back and forth in the kitchen. Quite often the field mice would leave the woods and enter in through the basement, climb up the water pipes into the upstairs kitchen to look for food. This particular night their sounds were noticeably louder and the running more frequent, as if they were playing games. I didn't dare go into the kitchen to investigate, and neither did Betty. The stillness of the night, the sounds from the television, and the scampering feet of the mice soon lulled us both to sleep.

I don't know how much time had passed when I felt smoke stinging my eyes and nose. I found it difficult to pull myself out of this strange sleep I was in; opening my eyes was a chore. I began coughing uncontrollably, which brought my heavy eyelids open. I pushed myself up from the couch with my hands, as I struggled to get to my feet. Billowing smoke had begun to fill the room. I stumbled to the kitchen doorway where I saw flames of fire lashing out from under the kitchen sink. As quickly as I could, I ran over to Betty screaming for her to get up, but she didn't budge. I frantically pulled on her arms, dragged her off the couch onto the hardwood floor. Hitting the floor with a thud brought her to her senses. Confused and bewildered, she found strength to get up.

"The kitchen's on fire!" I yelled to her. "We've gotta get out of here!".

We both scrambled for the dark bedroom, yelling to the children to wake up. By now the flames were leaping into the sitting area, the only way out would be through the front door. We had to work fast. Betty hurriedly pulled the blanket from the bed and wrapped Sam in it and headed for the living room door yelling to me to grab Jacob. He wanted to lie back down, but I yanked hard on his arm and told him to run out as fast as he could, because the house was on fire. Betty rushed the smaller siblings out to the night air coughing and wheezing and crying. In the darkness, I tripped over some shoes in the bedroom and fell to the floor in the open doorway, allowing more smoke to enter my lungs.

"Come on, Deedra, what's taking you so long?" Betty screamed back to me, but I couldn't lift myself up. "Fire! Fire! Somebody help us!" I could hear my sister yell. She ran back into the house to find me. I was lying in a heap on the floor, barely breathing. She grabbed both my arms and pulled me with all her might out to the porch, hoisted me up, and stumbled down the steps with me in tow— we both collapsed with exhaustion to the ground. I was coughing uncontrollably. The night air felt like a splash of cold water on my face, I began to inhale and exhale deeply, which slowly began to expel the smoke in my lungs and bring me back to my senses. By then, Mr. & Mrs. Burnside emerged from the basement still half asleep. The neighbor next door ran over in her nightgown screaming that she had called the fire department. I could vaguely hear the peel of fire engines in the distance. (We were later told that Mrs. Cott had called the fire department first. I wondered how she knew about the fire so quickly.) The clanging of the fire bells got closer and closer. It wasn't long before firemen were jumping out of a red shiny truck, pulling hard on a flat mossy green hose. The only fire hydrant was on the avenue, so they had to work quickly to get the hose hooked up and run the line back to our house. A couple of paramedics pulled up in an ambulance and ran to our aid. Thank goodness everyone was OK.

For thirty minutes, the firemen vigorously sprayed water on the house until they were sure they had finally extinguished the blaze. They gingerly climbed the stairs and walked carefully through the kitchen to inspect the damage. According to their report, the floor, the cabinets, the kitchen sink were all charred and burned, all ruined. A couple of field mice were lying on the floor dead. The firemen had no answer to how the house could've caught fire, only speculations. They were just thankful that the gas stove was in the corner on the opposite side and the flames didn't reach it. I remember that the pilot light had gone out earlier and I had relit it, otherwise, there could have been an explosion from escaping gas. The paramedics asked where our parents were. We explained that my father was working overtime at the mill and the one time our mother went out to see a movie, this had to happen. They suggested that we all sleep over at the next-door neighbors' until morning. By then, hopefully, the smoke would have died down.

About a half hour later, my mother arrived back home. Surprised to see the fire truck, the paramedics, and the neighbors standing around her children, she bounded out of the back seat of the car before it came to a stop. She was even more shocked that the house had caught fire. As expected, my mother felt guilty about leaving us home alone. It took some coaxing from Betty and me to assure her that this probably would have happened any way. She was more thankful that we were all alive and safe. She heartedly thanked the neighbors for looking after us by calling the fire department. The firemen explained to her that it was not safe to go into the house to spend the night. So, the one in charge gave her an ygen mask so she could go inside to get a few things to take to the neighbor next door where we would spend the night. She left a note on the front door to caution Bud and my father not to go inside, but to come next door where we were staying.

I laid my head on the neighbor's clean soft pillow. All kinds of thoughts swarmed inside my head. *Who had set that fire--the field mice playing with a box of matches? Or was it the ghost who seemed to take a delight in setting fires? The Cotts' fire? Did HE try to kill them too, or was it just me IT was after?* We could forget about being home for the holiday. Thank goodness the flames didn't reach the woods. It wasn't long before I fell into a deep sleep from sheer exhaustion.

****

Chapter Eight
In the Attic

January 1971 It is too bad that a tragedy had to happen before my parents felt the need to move away from that hideous place. The kitchen had been ruined and the smoke still hadn't completely settled in the upstairs. The fire didn't affect the landlords' quarters, so they were told to stay put in their underground world. But our whole family would have to find another place to live. No one was happier than I that we were finally moving away from McKinley Street, from the Trepples, but most of all, from the Ghost. I hoped that *He* had been burned up in the fire too.

Walter Pope was not a happy camper, though. Finding a vacant house in that town would be next to impossible. Usually people lived in the same place for years and years. In fact, they often died of old age in the house they raised their kids in. Sometimes owners would rent out a portion of their house after their children had grown up and moved out, which explains why the upstairs on McKinley Street was available. After the Burnsides' only son had been drafted into the Army, they had moved into the basement in order to rent the upstairs to help add on to their retirement money, which wasn't a lot. As our luck would have it, we found a small attic apartment about a mile away, one block west of McKinley Street. The space was cramped and hot, but at least we were all safe and sound. So here we were, in the attic of someone else's house. It had a queen bed, one night stand, and an old mattress on the floor where the boys slept. Betty and I were able to snuggle in the bed with our parents. We had limited use of the kitchen, and had to walk down into the basement to use the guest bathroom.

I didn't think it was the worst conditions, at least now we talked to each other more and became closer in a sweet sort of way. *More importantly*, I thought, *I don't have to sleep on the outside of the bed anymore.* Ah-h, sleep filled nights, who could ask for more. It was okay that I had to start a new school and learn new friends. As shy as I was, I was willing to make the best of it. Bud, on the other hand, got to keep going to his old school. My father would drop him off in the mornings at the Burnsides' house so he could feed the chickens and the dogs, which they allowed him to do. After school he had a long walk home, but he didn't care. It gave him more time to stretch his legs and less time to be cramped up in someone else's attic. But for me, things were going great. For the first time since my family moved to Indiana, I was really happy.

Chapter Nine
The Decision

March 1971 Three months passed by quickly. We were settled in our new school and had made a few new friends. Although my mother's distant cousin (fourth removed) was very generous to us with her home, my father had grown weary of our cramped living conditions. Every weekend he tried desperately to find another vacant house so we could move, but there were none to be had, at least not big enough to accommodate all seven of us *and* our animals. Seeing him so unhappy made all of us very jittery. Sometimes I would hear him late at night discussing our situation with my mother.

One night in particular, I was awakened by low voices. Rarely did I hear my parents argue, and when they did, they would go in their bedroom and shut the door so that we couldn't see or hear them so angry. Since there was no bedroom to retreat to, I could hear every word clearly, so I listened. My father said he had found a vacant flat three blocks away, but it was just big enough for him and the boys. He suggested that my mother could continue to stay in the attic with the girls, and the boys could stay with him— that Bud would have to look after them after school until he came home from work. Then we would all get together on the weekends at one or the other place. My mother challenged the idea; that it was ridiculous for him to want to jump ship so soon, and how dare he think of splitting the family up. I was devastated; the thought of the family splitting up was unimaginable. I felt the urge to scream out at him, *No, daddy, no!* I cupped my hands over both ears and squeezed my eyelids tight to hold back the tears that were already starting to sting. Slowly the tears quietly trickled down my cheeks on their own. I don't know when I finally fell back asleep.

The next morning I didn't dare let on to what I had overheard. Thank goodness my father had already gone to work, which meant I didn't have to risk an early morning confrontation with him. I mechanically got ready for school. I ate breakfast in silence, kissed my mother goodbye and headed out the door. On the way to school, Betty walked ahead of me with one of her friends, while I lagged behind, deep in my thoughts about what I could do to help. Neither of us noticed the open gate ahead of us. Without warning, two snarling dogs rushed out to the icy sidewalk snapping and yelping. Their long toenails couldn't get any traction on the cold ice-covered ground, so they began slipping and sliding on the pavement. Betty and her friend stumbled through the snow out into the street yelling at me to do the same, but the snow was so deep on the side of the walkway where I was, that I fell into a heap. Just as the dogs were about to get their footage to pounce on me, a lady came from inside the house yelling at them to stop and come back in the house. In that same instance, they tried to stop but continued to slide aimlessly on the ice. Gingerly, they slowly retreated to their yard. Before she shut the door, she apologized to us but didn't offer to help. My sister and her friend came over to help me up out of the snow, but they slipped on the icy walkway and fell in themselves.

When we finally arrived at school, we were late, wet, cold and crying. Instead of going to our classes, the assistant principal insisted that we sit by a space heater in her office to get warm and dry. She helped us empty the snow from our boots and hung our overcoats on a hanger in the hallway to dry. My cozy world was suddenly falling apart.

Decision Maker

I want to be a wise decision
maker, no matter what it takes
I want to think of others in spite
of my personal aches
Be a giver not just take, as a
flowing river not a placid lake

Decisions are sometimes hard to
form in your mind
Decisions can often take a long time
Decisions can take you forward
or leave you behind

I felt half responsible for us having to move in the first place. All that night, I was thinking of a plan to keep the family together, which would prove to be the most difficult decision that I had ever made. But I knew I had to go through with it. If I didn't, the possibility loomed that our family might never see each other again. I talked my plan over with Betty and swore her to secrecy. She agreed, because the idea of us splitting up made her feel weak. She gave me her best wishes and a low-keyed send off. I dressed warmly in my coat, mittens, and wool scarf and headed out the door telling my mother that I would be out back playing. Instead, I darted through an alley and headed for my destination. The long trek to the Burnsides, to the house on McKinley Street was grueling. Again thoughts swirled around in my head telling me that this was not my problem to solve, that surely my father would think of something. But he *had* thought of something—to split up the family. I couldn't bear to think about it anymore, I had to go forth with my plan.

The frost nipped at my fingers through the gloves, my toes started to tingle too. The frost biting my fingers and toes was not as painful as the slow hole that was being dug in my heart. I was almost there, just one more block. I could already see Mrs. Burnside bent over pushing a shovel full of snow from the driveway. I had not been back to that house to see her since the move. Quietly I approached the elderly woman. She saw me before I could speak.

"Deedra, what brings you here?" Mrs. Burnside asked curiously. Did you come all the way here alone?"

"Hello, Mrs. Burnside. Yes, my mother doesn't know that I'm here. We have this problem—I heard that you had a *For Rent* sign for the Upstairs—Bud had told me about it when he last came to feed the chickens.I asked her if I could speak with her for a few minutes. She stopped shoveling the snow to invite me in the basement for some hot chocolate. I had only been in the basement once when we had first moved upstairs, it seemed dreary and dark. I sat at the small dinette table and slowly drank the hot drink. An hour later feeling fully confident that I had done the right thing, I left for home. Three days later, my whole family moved back to the house on McKinley Street—the house with the ghost. I was willing to do whatever it took for us to be together, even if it meant living in a haunted house again. Besides, it had a new smell to it. The kitchen had been fixed, there was a new refrigerator and sink, and parts of the kitchen floor had been replaced as well. *Maybe it wouldn't squeak now*, I thought. But best of all, my father was smiling again, which made all of us very happy. I gladly let Betty sleep on the inside of the bed by the wall. After all, my sister *had* saved my life. That first night I slept until morning without incident.

Chapter Ten
IT's Back

April 1971 It didn't take long after we'd settled in that the footsteps *started up* again, but I knew I couldn't *start up* my complaining again to Betty or to my mother. That would be too selfish of me, so I chose to grin and bear it. At least I pretended to grin, but my insides were being ripped apart. I had come to dread nighttime now more than ever before. Not only did I feel afraid, I felt trapped.

School became my place of refuge. There I could mix and mingle with my old friends and chat about girl things. I told them about how much I hated going to the other school, about the dogs running from the yard, and about living in an attic. Unfortunately, when it came time to sit still to listen to my teacher, I couldn't keep my eyes open. Helplessly, I began catnapping when a classmate was giving an oral report, or when I was reading a book. Sometimes I would go into a deep sleep. Miss Engle had seen enough.

"Give this note to your mother. She needs to know that you're no longer taking an interest in your school work," she reprimanded me. Why, every time I look up you're sleeping, which is so out of character for you, Deedra," my teacher continued. I hate to have to do this, but I'll need to talk to your mother to see if she's aware of this and to see what can be done about it."

I dreaded the fact that I would have to confront my mother after all. I took my time walking home, trying to think of a different story to tell her. Maybe I could convince her that I was so bored in school that I would fall asleep to keep my sanity. Or that I was so content to be back in Miss Engle's class that her sweetness lulled me to sleep. I knew that Clara Pope was much too clever to fall for any of my weak excuses for *sleeping on the job.* Reluctantly, I gave the note to her as soon as I arrived home. She read it slowly.

"Sleeping in class? Why have you been sleeping in class, Deedra?" my mother asked. You know how important school is. You need to be listening *not* sleeping, that's why you go to bed at night--to sleep!"

"Mama, I try to sleep at night, but—never mind, I don't want to talk about it, please," I begged my mother to drop the conversation. I promised that I would do better, but she persisted.

"No, we *will* talk about it! What on earth is going on with you, young lady?"

"Mama, the ghost is back!" I blurted out choking back the tears. IT's come back to haunt me at night. I know you don't believe me, and I didn't want to bother you about it, but 'IT' won't let me sleep!" I began to cry uncontrollably.

My mother threw up both her hands in disgust and walked out of the room. I wished she had hugged me and told me that everything would be all right; instead she left me there bawling my eyes out. I knew then that I had to confront this demon myself--*alone.*

Chapter Eleven
Telling Books

"Excuse me, ma'am, but do you have any books on ghosts?" I asked the school librarian. She looked up over her horn-rimmed glasses and cocked her head to one side.

"Why would you want a book on ghosts?" she answered me with a question.

"I–I'm doing a research paper on them. I thought it would be an interesting topic to write about in my English class," I lied. I didn't want anyone to know why I really wanted to find a book, any book for that matter, on ghosts.

"We may have one or two back there in the Mystery section," the librarian said dryly.

I thanked Mrs. Quill and walked to the back of the library. Slowly I ran my fingers over the spine of each book, carefully reading every single title. I selected the four books that seemed ghostly— *The World Unknown, Darkness Before Day, The Casperian Theory, and The Presidents Cursed.* I took them over to a wooden table in a far corner of the room and began reading the back cover of each book.

The World Unknown was first. It was about testimonies of people who had witnessed unexplained strange occurrences in their houses. Each person told in detail how a nightly stalker would creep into their rooms and make eerie unexplainable noises. They told of how their dogs or cats would react to sights that were only visible to them. They even experienced having whole conversations with them, asking them why they are still lurking around? Or, what are they looking for?

The Darkness Before Day was about an elderly couple who had moved on the outskirts of town to get away from everyone. They told of mysterious happenings that went on just before the break of dawn over and over again in their Victorian cottage. The reasons why were known only to the dead. The husband eventually hanged himself, and the wife was taken to an asylum for the mentally ill.

The Casperian Theory goes about to prove that ghosts do exist in the underworld, and that they can communicate with the living in ways that humans can't communicate with each other. A nondenominational minister, Reverend Thaddeus Casper, had studied the occult for years, and concluded that ghosts are in a holding ground until they can pass on to the other side. He had actually located wandering spirits and helped them to move on to the other world that they sought after.

Finally, *The Presidents Cursed* was about how that every twenty or so years, one or another president would die or be assassinated while in office. No one could explain these unheralded events. The curse was eventually broken.

I couldn't risk taking more than one book home at a time. I couldn't chance Jacob or Sam's curiosity to get the best of them, then my fool-proof plan would be foiled for sure. For starters, I held on to *The World Unknown* and placed the other three back on the shelf. When I went up to the checkout desk, Mrs. Quill asked to hear again the reason that I needed a book on ghosts. I lied again. Little did I know that I would find the answers to my problem in those four books–*how to repel ghosts.*

Telling Books

If I couldn't read, I would be lost
in a world of mysteries
If I couldn't read, I'd be like a
dead tree standing in a green forest
If I couldn't read, who would take
me places I've never been?
If I couldn't read, how would I
educate myself about things
that I fear?
If I couldn't read, how would I set
my mind free?

For the next two weeks, I would go to the after-school library to pull another book from the shelf with a yellow legal pad and three pencils in tow. Each time Mrs. Quill would look at me with a quizzical expression as I led myself to the back of the library to the wooden table in the corner. One book at a time, I would take notes as I read, looking for clues that would help me solve this mysterious puzzle. I was secretly formulating my master plan to rid our family of that ghastly uninvited intruder—before *IT* got rid of me first. By the time I got to the fourth book, *The Presidents Cursed*, I went up to Mrs. Quill to check it out. Her book-worm antenna didn't seem to think that it would be about ghosts. She commented that the curse was broken a long time ago anyway.

When I got home, I sat on the back porch steps, and eagerly began to read about all those presidents who had died while in office. I was curious to learn why. I was even more curious that I now lived in a town with streets named after almost all thirty four of the presidents. The book turned out to be more than I expected. I thought it would just have facts and dates and events recorded about each president, but surprisingly it went into greater detail about the underlying mysteries surrounding their deaths. There was even a chapter on how to rid your house of evil spirits. Although I couldn't see the correlations to dead presidents, this book turned out to have a lot more answers than I realized. I became worried. If I was to pull off my plan, I would need a helper, someone who I could trust not to tell; someone who would be equally skillful and discreet as I was in order to make it work. After all, I was going to exorcise a ghost.

I was proud of how brave this new knowledge had made me feel. I already knew who I would ask for help.

Chapter Twelve
The Plan

May 1971 "Are you crazy!" Convincing a teenage brother to wait until midnight on a Saturday to drive you down through the city at twenty miles an hour was like pulling a crocodile's back teeth. I was already prepared for my brother's response.

"I can't really talk about it now or else it will break the spell. I just need you to say you'll do it and not tell mama or daddy. Please-se-se!" I pleaded with my brother.

"You actually think I'm going to drive you through town at twenty miles an hour, stopping long enough for you to sprinkle grave dust and steel ashes on the street. Dee, you've lost your mind!" Bud's eyes were stretched wider than I'd ever seen them.

"No, I haven't lost my mind. I've been reading these books on ghosts and stuff. Bud, I'm convinced that there really is another world that we can't see but can feel their presence. At least consider doing this for me," I continued to plead my case.

There was a long silence before my brother spoke again. "Let's just say I'm considering it, but it takes gas to pull this little escapade off," he concluded as if to say he would do it if I put extra gas in his car.

"I've got some babysitting money that I saved up, Bud. That is the least of my worries." I slowly bent both knees to the floor and clasped my hands to my heart.

"Deedra, I never thought I'd be telling this, last weekend when Dad took Mama and you guys to the movies and I stayed here to type my term paper, I heard some footsteps walking through the kitchen. I thought it was the rain hitting against the windows, but rain doesn't make the floors squeak. I tried to shrug it off, but it was so creepy that I got my jacket and took off to Scottie's house until I thought you guys would be back. Hey, I'm starting to feel uneasy around here myself. But if I do this crazy stunt, and that's a *big if*, you will be in my debt when I need a favor or two."

"Bud, I'll do whatever you want, no job is off limits," I eagerly responded.

"I just remembered—"

My brother instantly came up with a job for me, "Saturday I want to go shoot some early morning hoops with Scottie. I'll need you to collect the eggs from the chicken coop."

"Bud, you know how insulting that banter rooster of yours is, he'll never let me near those hens or the coop," I whined.

"Are you the same kid who just told me you'd do anything I want if I helped you pull this midnight thing off?

"Okay, okay!" I put my hands over my ears to drown out *his* bantering. "I'll do it!"

Chapter Thirteen
Exorcising a Ghost

Saturday couldn't come fast enough. I had a lot of preparations to do in order to pull off my plans. I got my daddy's huge steel mill gloves and boots and shook all of the steel dust I could muster into a small brown paper bag and hid it in the pantry for later on that night. Then I walked about five blocks to Miser's Cemetery on Grant Street, a small old dilapidated unattended graveyard elevated about six feet above the sidewalk surrounded by a dirty stucco wall. I ascended the five or six steps to an old rusted iron gate that led to the entranceway. Weeds had grown around the ashy-gray gravestones, soda cans and paper cluttered the weeded area. But this was the gravesite where I'd find the same last names of the five presidents on my list, *presidents who had died while they were in office.*

On my last visit to the library, I had copied a map of the locations of the headstones so it wouldn't take me long to find them and carry out this mission. I gingerly scooped dirt from each grave, carefully pouring the contents into five different paper bags that I had labeled with each president's name. Although Ulysses S. Grant didn't die while in office, *The World Unknown* suggested getting dirt from a grave with the name of the street that the graveyard was on. Ironically, there was no headstone that bore the last name Grant. Anyway, I was happy that I had found all the others.

As quickly as my feet would carry me, I took off for home. I needed to gather the eggs from the coop before Bud got back from his basketball workout and start yelling and spoil my plan. When I reached Grover Cleveland Street, I darted through the woods to our backyard. I hid the paper bags behind the garage inside an old hollowed tree stump and covered them with some broken tree limbs and leaves. I caught sight of Charlie prancing around the backyard between the coop and the back stairs. He was curiously plucking at something on the ground. Not waiting for him to catch sight of me, I ran as fast as I could pass him and bounded up the back stairs to get one of daddy's gloves. I needed to put it on in case I had to fend myself from the rooster's fierce talons. I grabbed an apple from the pantry and two slices of bread.

"Char—lie!" I called out to him in a melodious tone. "Char—lie, I have a nice red, juicy apple for you. Come and get it!" I lured the rooster over away from the coop.

Charlie loved to eat rare finds. Apples, his favorites, were not easy to come by. His curiosity got the best of him, slowly he approached me; cautiously prancing. I had his attention. Once he got close enough I knelt down and rolled the apple all the way to the other end of the back yard. Forgetting about his harem, he skittered after it. I pulled the bread apart into small pieces and quickly scattered the crumbs all over the ground. The hens came running from every direction and began busying themselves by pecking at the bread. I ran over to the coop and began gingerly picking up egg after egg from inside, placing them in a straw basket that Bud kept on top of the wire pen. Just as I was about to get the last egg, Charlie looked up from his half-eaten apple, his red crown stood up on his head as he realized that he had been tricked from his watch. He spread his wings and began flapping wildly in the breeze, his feathered body lifted in the air. When he started his charge at me, I zigzagged through the frightened hens that were now running in every direction and ran to the back stairs. I made it to the top without breaking one egg. Charlie knew he had been outwitted.

The rest of the day I waited and thought a lot and slept. I waited for ten thirty when everyone was fast asleep. I thought my plan through over and again to make sure I hadn't forgotten an important detail. Fully dressed, I slipped into bed to get some much needed sleep, so that I could be fresh and alert for our midnight caper.

An hour later, I eased out of bed making sure I didn't wake Betty. I tiptoed to the bathroom, washed my face and swished warm water around in my mouth, then spat it out. I checked on my big brother, who was already pulling on his sneakers. At eleven o'clock that night, Bud and I tiptoed out of the house. Betty was still fast asleep; Dad's snoring was so loud we were sure that no one heard us. I grabbed the bag with the steel dust in it from the pantry. Bud slowly pulled open the creaky back door; cautiously we crept down the dark stairs. As still as we could, we walked towards the back of the garage, making sure we didn't disturb the roosting chickens and Charlie. I collected all the bags from their secret place. Bud had left the car near the edge of the woods so that the sudden roar of the engine wouldn't wake up everyone. We started down the avenue headed several blocks east. My feat was to sprinkle steel ashes (something that represented why we moved into this town) mixed with grave dirt of *'dead presidents'* on the streets of the presidents who had died while in office. The first stop was William H. Harrison Street.

"Bud, slow down, slow down!" I quietly yelled. Bud reluctantly eased his foot off of the gas pedal, still thinking it was a ridiculous idea but hoping for a miracle. I hung my head and hands out of the window, while chanting some special words, and then I emptied the contents of the brown bag labeled Harrison in the middle of the intersection. I repeated this as I came to each designated street, at each intersection. Zachary Taylor's death was questionable but four days after July 4, 1850, he mysteriously died. I didn't dare take a chance on history's mistake. I dropped his designated contents on the intersection. Next, on to Abraham Lincoln Street, then James Garfield Street. We crossed McKinley Street but didn't stop. Bud headed on down to Warren G. Harding Street to stop at the intersection and wait while I gingerly poured the potion onto the pavement. Then we headed to Franklin D. Roosevelt Street. I had two more bags left. I made sure to pick up the one with Roosevelt on it and carefully poured the mixture onto the intersection. Finally, we headed back home to William McKinley Street. I took the last bag, made sure the name on the bag matched its namesake. I repeated the ritual for the last time.

Bud insisted that I had forgotten one president, but I told him that I had made sure that there was a bag marked for each fallen president. He still persisted with his hunch that I was forgetting someone, and I persisted that I hadn't.

Two o'clock in the morning, I was satisfied that the job had been completed. We were both too exhausted to leave the car parked behind the woods and walk, so Bud drove up to the house, turned the ignition off and allowed it to coast into the driveway. It was not long before I heard soft snoring from the boys' room, Bud had fallen fast asleep. But I didn't have the luxury of sleep, I would have to lie in wait for IT to appear, then I would make my next move. I felt my eyelids droop without my permission. Overcome with exhaustion, I soon felt myself falling fast asleep too.

Chapter Fourteen
Waiting

Early in the morning, the sun was still low on the horizon, hot rays streamed between the curtains burning my eyelids. I covered my face from the intense heat with my hand. What time was it? Who let me sleep so late? I could hear my mama in the kitchen singing one of her favorite Sunday hymns, while the aroma of homemade biscuits waffled from the oven. Bacon sizzled in the wrought iron frying pan atop the stove, while Clara Pope vigorously beat eggs in a bowl. I looked over at Betty, but her spot was empty. The two younger siblings were gazing into the TV at a favorite cartoon show. I groaned out loud.

"Get up sleepy head," Betty called out to me from the bathroom. "Why are you so tired? Had a hot date last night?" I wondered if she had heard us after all when we left–or when we came back, I didn't dare answer her. I pulled myself from the couch/bed to poke my head in the bedroom; Bud was still laid out snoring profusely. I was so proud of how he had handled everything, he was a champ.

After breakfast, I settled down to finish reading the last book I had brought home from the library, *The*

Presidents Cursed. The book seemed to open up on its own to page 66. *Ulysses Simpson Grant was an American general and the 18th president of the United States—*

Carefully I allowed my mind to relive the night before, seeing Bud slowly stop at each intersection. I had thrown the contents of each bag onto the right intersection; I had made sure nothing was left out. Every step of my plan had been carried out without fail. I felt so sure of myself, yet I became a little unsure as I read the words on the page.

Why is this so significant? I pondered. If Grant didn't die in office, then why would I need to stop at that street? My mind went back to Bud, how he insisted that I had forgotten someone. But I had done my homework; I must have gone over that plan a hundred times in my head. Trying to shake the cloud of doubt that was creeping into my fool-proof plan, I continued to read. Most of the information was about Grant's tenure in office and the honors he received for his part in the Civil War.

"Bud! You need to get up now, your breakfast is already cold, "Mama called from the kitchen. She was clearing the table and putting things away so she could begin her preparation for an early Sunday dinner.

"Deedra, please wake your sleepy-head brother up, he's sleeping way too long."

I went into the room with a warm wet face towel and placed it over my brother's face. He suddenly sat up in bed wondering what time it was.

"It's already noon. I brought your breakfast for you. You just stay in bed as long as you need to." I reminded him not to say a word about last night.

For the rest of the day I read a lot, took a walk in the woods then waited again for night to fall—anticipating the appearance of the ghost. I was ready to get rid of this creature once and for all. It would take another two weeks before I got my wish.

Ghost Notes

Chapter Fifteen
The Ghastly Truth

June 1971 Er—r-r! The backdoor was being slowly pushed open. This time I couldn't stay in bed and succumb to shivering and holding my breath, I would have to contend with this beast face to face. Only then would I know if IT was real or just a figment of my imagination. Somehow I had developed nerves of steel. Slowly I turned the covers back and quietly crept out of bed, making sure I didn't disturb Betty. Luckily the moon provided enough light in the room to keep me from bumping into anything. My heart pounding loudly, I continued my push for the truth. Lowly, softly, steadily I crept into the kitchen to the doorway of the pantry. I gasped, stopping dead in my tracks.

There in the shadows was a tall, well-dressed, dark translucent body wearing a long black trench coat and a Stetson hat, a dark silk scarf hung loosely around its neck. He had dark bushy brows and a large protruding nose. He bared uneven sharp teeth. His eyes were ablaze. In his hands, he clutched a long shiny machete. Slowly IT hoisted both arms high in the air above his head, ready to destroy me with the weapon. I started to hyperventilate uncontrollably. I knew I would have to reach deep into my inner self to overcome my fear and take control. My throat allowed me to gasp out the repetitive chants that I had memorized from the *Casperian Theory*.

"Steel ashes and grave dust, aligned on the parallel cusp! Steel ashes and grave dust aligned on the parallel cusp! Steel ashes and grave dust—" I got louder and louder with each chant.

IT stood motionless, the machete still looming above my head as if some force held onto his hands, rendering them immovable. I continued the chants. Breathless, I broke away and ran into the living room to wake up my sister and the rest of the family for them to come and see. Bud had already come running out from the room with mama behind him. My father came out later upset with the entire ruckus.

"What the dickens is going on, Deedra?" he yelled. Why aren't you in bed asleep?"

"Daddy, it was him! I saw him, the ghost! I saw him! He's in the pantry!" I screeched.

My father went in the pantry to look around. He checked the back door lock, everything was still intact. Just as he was about to put his daughter in her place, he spotted a strange black scarf lying on the floor. Curious, he picked it up and brought it in the living room where we all were waiting. There was steel mill ashes and dirt on the scarf. Without a word said, he shook his head and retreated back into the bedroom.

My mother tried to console me, telling me that everything would be OK. Bud and the others looked on in amazement. Daddy returned to the living room with his robe and slippers with the scarf still in his hand. He uneasily lowered himself down in his arm chair and began to talk. He explained that he knew some things about the occult and the strange occurrences that went on around the house. He told us that the black silk scarf meant there was a presence of evil that made its way through the back door.

Steel Mill Ashes and Grave Dust

Ashes of steel mixed with grave dust
Will rid you of your horrid curse
You must ride backwards in an old sedan
Dropping the mixture as evenly as you can

An old wives' tale once was told
Of a ghastly creature ever so bold
Who made nightly visits on an unsuspecting soul

Night after night to return from the grave
Refusing to resist his gluttonous crave
To live again in a house that he once occupied
To sleep again in a room where he had died—

Chapter Sixteen
Leaving McKinley Street

The next day our family started to pack up everything to make another big move, not knowing where we would go. But one thing we knew for sure, this time we wouldn't return. My mother had heard about a house that would be vacant in three days, so she left in haste to pay the owner a visit. We all kept our fingers crossed that she would come back with good news. My father went downstairs to tell the Burnsides our plan to move. He knew that he hadn't given them the required thirty days notice, but strangely enough the Burnsides understood, they were reluctant to stay there at the house as well. In fact, they admitted that when we had moved away the first time, they heard unexplainable footsteps at night above their heads. Since they both were retired, they decided to put the house up for sale and move into a high rise in the downtown area for the elderly. By the weekend, that old green dilapidated house on McKinley Street had been abandoned. Our family and the Burnsides had moved into our 'new' homes. Now the ghostly intruder could have his beloved house.

A strange thing happened just a month later— the house caught fire again, and this time burned down to the ground. My father drove me by there to see if all my fears had been destroyed with the fire. I wanted to say out loud that I hoped the ghost had burned in the fire too, but I kept that to myself. When he was about to back the car out of the driveway, he could see Mrs. Trepple emerge from her house beckoning for him to come over to her. She came out to the road and stood to wait for him. He curiously backed the car out into the street and pulled up alongside her. He rested his foot on the brakes, hoping that she would get the hint that he didn't plan to stay long. Completely ignoring me, she leaned over the window and spoke softly to him, making sure that I didn't hear her conversation. I could tell she was trying to explain something to him. My father looked at her in awe as she continued to whisper. After several minutes, he thanked her, lifted his foot off the brakes and drove off.

I didn't bother to wave goodbye to her, because my focus was only on him, wanting desperately to know what kind of secrets Mrs. Trepple had kept from us. But I was not allowed to ask grown folks what they had been discussing. So I waited, hoping that my father would volunteer to tell me about her strange conversation. I almost jumped out of my skin when he began to tell me everything she had just said.

Mrs. Trepple had explained that there was a first owner of the house long before the Burnsides. He had lived upstairs and used the basement for storage. He suddenly became ill and was told that he didn't have long to live. He didn't have any family who was willing to care for him, so she and Mrs. Cott took turns cooking his food and cleaning his house, and even got the boys to mow his grass. Of course, he paid them handsomely for their services. A few days before he died, he called them both together to tell them about his will; that he would leave the property in their care. They could either sell it or rent it out, and split the proceeds. However, there was one catch—they had to tell the new tenants or new owners who the first owner was. To complicate matters, they had to tell them that he had died there, and more importantly, that he would never leave his beloved house, even after death.

Because of the fear and greed that Mrs. Trepple and Mrs. Cott both shared, they certainly had no intentions of disclosing his promise to pay unexpected visits there, knowing it would be hard to get someone to move into the house once they knew that it was haunted. After his death, the two also conspired not to tell any prospective buyers or renters that he was the true owner. When the Burnsides bought the house, they were told that Mrs. Trepple and Mrs. Cott had purchased the property together, which explains why the old man would pay unexpected visits to *their* houses as well.

"Thank goodness the fire didn't reach the woods," I said quietly to my father.

Conclusion

According to Wikipedia (Internet), **Fear** is an emotional response to threats and danger. Additionally, fear is related to the specific behaviors of escape and avoidance.

Overcoming your fear. Some experts say you should face your fears head on—taking small steps will help increase your confidence. Checking things out for yourself by asking questions, researching, and observing, will help dispel any myths that your mind may have conjured up. Getting the facts first will save unnecessary stress and anxiety. Change your way of looking oat life—things you can and can't see. Take command of the here and now. Don't allow your brain to over-analyze situations. Surrender your emotional one minute, one hour, and one day at a time and think positive thoughts more.

Did I tell you that we moved to a house on Grant Street—ironically across from Miserly Cemetery. Remember how Bud had argued with me about a president that I had forgotten? Well, I reread page 66, this time more carefully—*If you move to another presidential street, perhaps it would be wise to sprinkle dust on that street as well or else your ghostly stalker will find you and come back to pay you a few nightly visits.*

I wondered how my brother, Bud, knew to question me about that—

THE END

(Or is it only just getting started?)

THE YEAR FOR THE CHILD

It's the year for the child--
(An embryo in types and shadows
still feeling the warmth of the womb,
almost too shy for the light outside).

Although this vast universe can be cold
And sometimes stings your souls
It is a never-ending schoolmaster
Towards Divine Knowledge and Love...

Children, you must be ready writers--
Filling your journals with the
understanding of your youth,
Girding your loins with Wisdom
Obtained only through a sincere
heart and an open mind.

by edeth hamm

About The Author

Edeth Hamm has written a picture book about her dogs, a how-to-book on parenting and a curriculum guide for beginning teachers who are teaching 4th grade language arts. With a Master's degree in Elementary Education, a writing certificate from the Institute of Children's Literature in Connecticut, and over thirty years of teaching experience, she has a good handle on what children of ALL ages enjoy reading.